Johnny Appleseed

Tale retold by Bill Balcziak
Illustrated by Jason Millet

Adviser: Dr. Alexa Sandmann, Professor of Literacy,
The University of Toledo; Member, International Reading Association

COMPASS POINT BOOKS
Minneapolis, Minnesota

Compass Point Books
3722 West 50th Street, #115
Minneapolis, MN 55410

Visit Compass Point Books on the Internet at *www.compasspointbooks.com*
or e-mail your request to *custserv@compasspointbooks.com*

Editor: Catherine Neitge
Designer: Les Tranby

Library of Congress Cataloging-in-Publication Data
Balcziak, Bill, 1962-
  Johnny Appleseed / written by Bill Balcziak; illustrated by Jason Millet.
      p. cm. — (The Imagination series: Tall tales)
Summary: Presents the life story of John Chapman, whose distribution of apple seeds and trees across the
Midwest made him a legend of tall tales and left a legacy still enjoyed today.
  ISBN 0-7565-0458-9 (hardcover)
  1. Appleseed, Johnny, 1774-1845—Juvenile literature. 2. Apple growers—United States—Biography—
Juvenile literature 3. Frontier and pioneer life—Middle West—Juvenile literature. [1. Appleseed, Johnny,
1774-1845. 2. Apple growers. 3. Folklore—United States. 4. Tall tales.] I. Title. II. Balcziak, Bill, 1962-.
Imagination series: Tall tales.
  SB63.C46 B36 2003
  634'.11'092—dc21   2002015117

Table of Contents

Dreaming of Destiny .4

On the Go Again 16

Saving a Wolf .20

Let's Be Friends 24

The Westward Journeys of Johnny Appleseed . . .28

Apple Muffins 29

Glossary 30

Did You Know? 30

Want to Know More? 31

Index 32

Dreaming of Destiny

In a small house in Massachusetts, a young man lay in bed every night dreaming of adventure. It was the late 1700s, and the United States was a young country. A whole continent was waiting to be explored. The young man had a feeling that a special destiny awaited him.

The young man's name was John Chapman. This is his story. Some of it is really true!

Some people thought John Chapman was a little strange. He was tall and skinny with long, tangled brown hair. He sometimes forgot to wear shoes—even in winter! His clothes never matched. John wore unusual hats. Sometimes he wore a moth-eaten top hat or an animal skin cap.

John always wore a smile, too.

In spite of his strange habits and clothes, people liked him.

When John Chapman was 20 years old, he decided to leave his home. He carried a few coins and some clothes in a pack and wore a cook pot for a hat. John didn't know where he was going, but he knew what direction to head. West! He would head west to the wild places.

His friends and neighbors said, "John, you're a crazy young man—there's Indians and bears that-a-way!" He didn't listen to them, though. He just started walking.

It wasn't long before he came to the start of the great forest and the valley of the Hudson River. This was where the towns and farms came to an end. This was where the real West began. Very few people had traveled this far. Young John Chapman knew there was a long, hard journey ahead.

There were no maps or signs to point John in the right direction. There weren't even any roads. He followed the Native American trails. He walked among the deer and the beaver, the hawks and the squirrels. He was lost much of the time.

Since he didn't have any special place to go, he didn't worry about it. He would walk until he got tired. Then he would find the biggest oak tree in the forest and lay down under it for a nap.

John Chapman loved trees. "Every tree has its own character," he used to tell people. He said that oaks were the strongest trees. Willows were lazy. They hung gently over streams and rivers, swaying in the wind. Pine trees were the protectors. They made a roof over the animals and plants on the forest floor.

He knew a little something about every tree, but his favorite was the apple tree. In fact, it was an apple tree—or rather, a whole orchard of apple trees—that saved John Chapman's life. But we're getting ahead of the story.

That first autumn of his journey, John Chapman was tired and hungry. The West seemed a million miles away. He was out of food. It was getting cold, and he couldn't find anything to eat. He was growing weaker every day.

The young man wandered through the forest, searching for something—anything—to eat. Suddenly, he found himself in a clearing. From the looks of it, he had walked onto a deserted farm site. There was nobody around. The only things growing in the fields were weeds. As John walked across those empty fields, he saw a beautiful sight at the edge of the clearing. It was an apple orchard. There were ten trees, heavy with fruit.

The trees were filled with big, red, juicy apples waiting to be picked. John Chapman figured since nobody lived there anymore, it might be OK if he took a few apples to eat. Nothing ever tasted better than those apples! John ate his fill.

When he finished his meal, John looked down at the apple cores on the ground. They had fallen from his hand and formed a pattern that looked like an arrow. Oh, my! John looked up at the sun and noticed that the arrow was pointing west. It was a sign!

At that exact moment, John Chapman decided he would line his path west with apple trees. "Then someday," he said to himself, "apple trees will point the way to the West!"

On the Go Again

John stayed at the farm and regained his strength. He ate apples every day and saved every seed. Soon his pack was stuffed with seeds. John knew it was time to start his mission. Each day, he planned his route and dreamed about fields filled with apple trees. When the weather warmed, he grabbed his pack full of seeds and put the old cook pot atop his head. He left the farm, never to return.

To his amazement, there were now many settlers traveling along

the same routes. The new United States government promised free land to those who wanted to go west. People jumped at the chance to own land there.

John Chapman made many friends along the way. He told the travelers he met about his vision of a land filled with apple trees. Sometimes they laughed at his story. Some people thought he was crazy. More and more people, however, wanted to hear what he had to say. He gave them seeds. He sold them seedlings. He offered advice on planting, growing, and harvesting apples from the trees.

Whenever he came to a farmhouse or clearing, he stopped his travels to plant a few dozen apple seeds in nice, neat rows.

One day, John Chapman was standing in a town square talking to some men about apples. A crowd gathered to hear his interesting stories. Suddenly, a boy called out, "You tell 'em, Johnny Appleseed!" The crowd roared with laughter.

The nickname stuck, and John Chapman became Johnny Appleseed. Whenever people saw the man with the cook pot on his head, they would cry out, "There goes Johnny Appleseed!"

People began to tell wild stories about Johnny Appleseed. The stories were told and retold by settlers, trappers, and soldiers. After so many retellings, it was hard to know which parts of the stories were true and which were made up. But since the stories were so much fun, nobody minded. (That's how tall tales get started.)

Saving a Wolf

One story took place during the cold, cold winter of 1808. Johnny was trying to sleep under the branches of an apple tree. It was dark and snowy. He could hear wolves in the nearby woods. They were howling at something. He got up, dusted the snow off his coat, and crept through the trees to see them better.

There were ten angry wolves circling something on the ground. It was a female lying on her side, breathing hard. Her front leg was caught in a large hunter's trap.

The wolves picked up Johnny's scent and turned toward him. But they did not attack. Instead, the wolves parted to let him through.

He slowly bent down to the trapped animal. She growled. He growled back to show her he wasn't afraid. He stroked her thick, warm fur and reached for her trapped leg. Then—and it was the strangest thing—she placed her other paw on Johnny Appleseed's hand. He took it as a sign she trusted him. He freed her leg. Instead of biting him, she began to lick his face!

The wolf became his faithful companion. One time, people said, she even traveled down a river with him on a giant block of ice. It was the spring of 1811, so the story goes. It had been another cold, hard winter. The Ohio River ice broke up late in the season. Huge chunks of ice raced along with the current. Folks warned Johnny to wait for warmer weather, but he wanted to push on.

Johnny told the wolf to stay put and he slid his canoe in the water. Then, he thought, why not float down the river *on* the ice?

So Johnny paddled out into the middle of the river and dragged his canoe onto the biggest piece of ice he could find.

The wolf swam out to Johnny. They stood shakily on the ice, trying to find their balance. Finally they got the hang of it and actually started to enjoy the ride. When they passed a small village, the people watching from the riverbank stared, their mouths hanging open in shock. The wolf howled and Johnny Appleseed waved his cook pot hat as they raced down the icy Ohio River.

Let's Be Friends

Over time, the stories became even more amazing. People still talk about the day Johnny faced down a group of angry Native Americans. He was helping a family plant an orchard of apple trees. Suddenly, a boy came running up, shouting about an Indian attack. "They're coming for a fight!" he cried, pointing toward the woods.

Johnny walked to the trees, hoping he could prevent a battle. As he moved into the woods, he spotted a Native American just

ahead. Then another, and another. There were a hundred Native Americans facing him. "Hello," he said softly, sticking out his hand. "I am Johnny Appleseed. I am your friend."

The Native Americans stared at him. They started to circle. The chief gave Johnny a mean, angry look. He shook his bow at Johnny and reached for an arrow. Then the chief paused. Johnny could see he was trying to decide what to do next. Johnny didn't want to wait for the answer.

He slowly reached into his pack and took a handful of apple seeds. Johnny tossed them in a circle around himself. The ground sparked where the seeds landed. There was a giant crack as the seeds turned into saplings. Just like that, the saplings grew and grew until they were nearly the size of full-grown apple trees. The branches shook as the trees started to bear fruit. In less than a minute's time, the seeds had exploded into grown trees full of big, ripe apples.

The Native Americans ran into the woods, terrified. After a few minutes they returned. They carefully picked some apples and tasted the fruit. More and more people joined in the feast. Finally, the chief himself came to Johnny and shook his hand. "You are our friend," he said.

It turns out those Indians were as hungry as Johnny. They sat together and ate their fill. They were friends from that day on.

And that's exactly what *might* have happened. True tale or tall tale, the legend of Johnny Appleseed is one of America's greatest stories. John Chapman might be gone, but his stories—and his trees—live on.

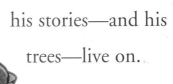

The Westward Journeys of Johnny Appleseed

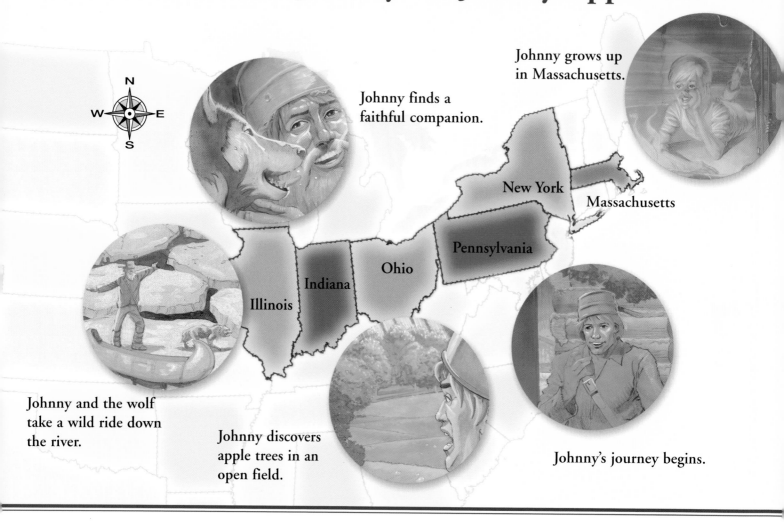

Johnny finds a faithful companion.

Johnny grows up in Massachusetts.

New York

Massachusetts

Pennsylvania

Ohio

Indiana

Illinois

Johnny and the wolf take a wild ride down the river.

Johnny discovers apple trees in an open field.

Johnny's journey begins.

The story of Johnny Appleseed is a great chapter in American history. It is based on the life of a man named John Chapman, a real explorer who lived more than 200 years ago. As a young man, Chapman wanted to see America. He headed west with nothing more than his clothes and a few coins. He traveled with the pioneers and lived with the Native Americans. He planted apple trees along the way, and this is how he got the nickname Johnny Appleseed. His story grew into a tall tale after being told and retold by many generations of Americans. Now, the legend of Johnny Appleseed is as big as the trees this great man left in his path.

Apple Muffins

Johnny Appleseed would have loved this recipe! You will, too. Makes twelve muffins.

2 cups flour
2 teaspoons baking powder
1/4 cup white sugar
1/2 teaspoon ground cinnamon
1/2 teaspoon salt

1 cup milk
1 egg, beaten
1/4 cup butter, melted
1 cup apple, peeled
  and chopped

Preheat oven to 400 degrees F. Be sure an adult helps you with the hot oven. Line twelve muffin cups with paper muffin liners. In a large bowl, stir together flour, baking powder, sugar, cinnamon, and salt. In another bowl, stir together milk, egg, and butter. Stir egg mixture into flour mixture just until combined. Stir in chopped apples. Spoon batter into muffin cups. Bake for 20 minutes or until a toothpick inserted into center of a muffin comes out clean.

Glossary

amazement—a feeling of surprise

companion—special friend

continent—one of the seven large land areas on Earth; they are Africa, Antarctica, Asia, Australia, Europe, North America, and South America

destiny—events that were meant to happen

harvesting—to pick ripe fruit, vegetables, or other crops

howling—the act of making a long, loud cry by an animal

Hudson River—a river that runs through the state of New York

legend—a story passed down through the years that may not be completely true

mission—a special job

nickname—a name used instead of someone's real name

Ohio River—a large river that flows through central North America

orchard—an area of land where fruit trees are planted

protector—someone or something that keeps you safe

regain—to get back

route—a plan to get from one place to another

sapling—a young tree

vision—a plan for the future

Did You Know?

There are more than 2,000 kinds of apples, but only a few kinds are sold in stores. Johnny Appleseed's favorite was said to be the green Rambo apple. Its first seeds were brought to North America from Sweden in the 1600s.

John Chapman was born on September 26, 1774, in Leominster, Massachusetts. The local historical society said his father, Nathaniel Chapman, was one of the Minutemen who fought in the Battle of Concord. Nathaniel later fought with the Continental army during the Revolutionary War.

John Chapman died on March 18, 1845. His gravesite is a national historic landmark. It is in Archer Park in Fort Wayne, Indiana.

30

Want to Know More?

At the Library

Kellogg, Steven. *Johnny Appleseed.* New York: William Morrow and Co., 1988.

Moses, Will. *Johnny Appleseed: The Story of a Legend.* New York: Philomel, 2001.

Osborne, Mary Pope. *American Tall Tales.* New York: Scholastic, 1991.

Spies, Karen. *Our Folk Heroes.* Brookfield, Conn.: The Millbrook Press, 1994.

On the Web

Treasure Treasure
http://www.treatures.com
To visit an interactive site that uses cartoon characters to focus on trees

Johnny Appleseed Picture Find
http://www.niehs.hih.gov/kids/apples.html
To find and color hidden pictures in a drawing of Johnny Appleseed

Through the Mail

American Forests' Historic Tree Nursery
8701 Old Kings Road
Jacksonville, FL 32219
1-800-320-TREE (8733)
http://www.historictrees.org/
To learn about trees grown from cuttings of a tree planted by John Chapman

On the Road

Johnny Appleseed Festival
Johnny Appleseed/Archer Parks
Fort Wayne, IN 46805
260/427-6003
http://www.johnnyappleseedfest.com
To visit the city where John Chapman is buried and attend an annual September festival in his honor

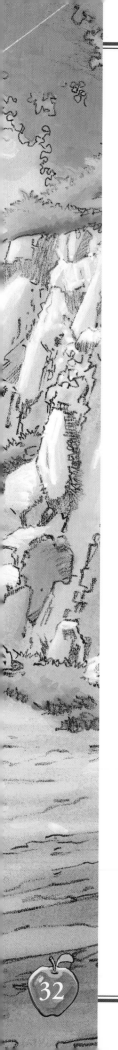

Index

animals, 10, 11, 20, 23
apple muffins (recipe), 29
apple seeds, 16, 17, 27
apple trees, 11, 13–14, 16, 17, 27
childhood, 4
clothes, 6, 28
food, 13, 16
hats, 6
Hudson River Valley, 8
Massachusetts, 4
Native Americans, 10, 24–25, 28
nickname, 18, 28

oak trees, 11
Ohio River, 22–23
pine trees, 11
recipe (apple muffins), 29
seeds, 16, 17, 27
settlers, 16–17, 18, 28
shoes, 6
tales, 18, 20, 22–25, 27
trails, 10
trees, 11, 13–14, 16, 17, 27
willow trees, 11
wolf companion, 20, 23

About the Author
Bill Balcziak has written a number of books for children. When he is not writing, he enjoys going to plays, movies, and museums. Bill lives in Minnesota with his family under the shadow of Paul Bunyan and Babe, the Blue Ox.

About the Illustrator
Since graduating from Chicago's American Academy of Art in 1993, Jason Millet has spent most of his time working in advertising. He has also designed T-shirts for the Chicago Bulls and Chicago's annual Blues Festival. This is his third children's book. Jason lives in Chicago.